Town Book Press
255 East Broad Street
Westfield, NJ 07090

♥A·Warthog

To our son
Nicholas Kirk Devlin

30th Anniversary Edition © 1998 by Town Book Press
Copyright © 1970 by Wende and Harry Devlin

Town Book Press
255 East Broad Street
Westfield, NJ 07090

Printed in Korea

10 9 8 7 6 5 4 3 2 1

Devlin, Wende.
        A kiss for a warthog / Wende and Harry Devlin. -- 1st Town Book
    Press ed.
            p.   cm.
        Summary: If the warthog destined for the Oldwick zoo had not had
    a mind of her own, the rival towns of Oldwick and Quimby might
    never have become friends.
        ISBN 1-892657-01-5
        [1. Warthog--Fiction. 2. Neighborliness--Fiction. 3. Humorous
    stories.] I. Devlin, Harry II. Title.
    PZ7.D49875Ki   1970b
    [E]--dc21
                                                    98-36370
                                                      CIP
                                                       AC

The town of Oldwick and the town of Quimby had always been rivals.

It wasn't for the sake of baking cakes that the ladies of Oldwick baked cakes. They baked cakes so their families would say, "That's a better cake than they can bake over in Quimby."

Oldwick baseball teams played baseball, not for the fun of playing baseball, but to beat the Quimby team.

4

Everything was done to best the other town, and that's why Allegra was on the high seas. Allegra was a warthog, and the whole town of Oldwick was anxiously awaiting her arrival.

The zoo in Oldwick had birds as fine as the birds in the zoo at Quimby, and logical Oldwickians thought their alligator was every bit as fierce as the alligator at Quimby. However, the Quimby zoo had a warthog–a great, whiskery, warted, walloping African warthog.

This hurt Oldwick's pride.

It had even been rumored that Oldwick's children had been seen in Quimby admiring the wonderful warthog.

"Why don't we have our own warthog?" the baker asked the taylor.

"Why don't we have our own warthog?" the citizens asked the mayor.

The mayor, who was immensely proud of his town, immediately telephoned Africa for a warthog. After a careful scanning of many warthogs, a fine female with bright eyes named Allegra was chosen for the trip.

Allegra enjoyed great popularity on her ocean voyage. Other passengers, after a bit of nudging, shared their deck chairs. Allegra was asked to share their fruit and candy.

After a while she became aware of shipboard custom and manners. She was usually first in line at the fire drill.

True, she never sat at the captain's table, but Allegra considered this a small oversight on the captain's part. At all other social events she was very much in demand. By the time the S.S. *Queen Victoria* docked at Oldwick, Allegra had almost forgotten that she was a warthog.

A great crowd met the S.S. *Queen Victoria.*
Aunts were there to greet uncles!
Mothers were there to greet children!
Even sisters were there to greet brothers!
A special zoo committee was there to greet Allegra.

At a whistled toot, the gates were opened, the gang-plank lowered, and everyone was suddenly kissing everyone.

Aunts kissed uncles!

Mothers kissed children!

And sisters even kissed brothers!

Allegra was the first to notice that nobody kissed Allegra. Second to notice was the captain of the S.S. *Queen Victoria*.

Captain Willoughby knew the nature of warthogs, He knew that warthogs are sensitive and very, very stubborn. Captain Willoughby looked worried.

Allegra took a very determined position on the gangplank and sat waiting for her welcoming kiss.

None came.

People on the ship shuffled about impatiently, but Allegra continued to sit on the gangplank waiting for her kiss.

"Somebody has to give the warthog a welcoming kiss," Captain Willoughby said.

The zoo committee, which was made up of the mayor, the fire chief, and a very important lady, shuffled and looked at their shoes. The fire chief turned to the mayor and said, "You kiss babies all the time."

The mayor turned pale green, and suddenly remembered he had an important council meeting.

The fire chief looked nervous and sniffed the air.

"I smell smoke, I think," he cried.

They turned to Mrs. Brussell-Jones.

"You love animals," they said.

"I feel faint–the crowds, you know," she said.

The passengers became impatient.
"A kiss for the warthog!" "A kiss for Allegra!"
the zoo committee regrouped behind a pile of trunks.
"I will *not* draw straws," said Mrs. Brussell-Jones.
"Count me out," said the fire chief.
The crowd grew noisier.

His honor the mayor, white and shaken, looked grim.
At last he said, "Pride be hanged. There's but one thing
to do. We'll borrow Quimby's warthog."

The zoo committee looked shocked. Then they all
looked at Allegra awaiting her kiss. "It's the only way!"
they said in unison.

Soon Oldwick's fire engine, with the committee aboard, was roaring and clanging its way to Quimby. When they arrived, the mayor of Oldwick went straight to the office of the mayor of Quimby. Quimby's mayor was moved by the committee's desperate plea. Surprisingly, he agreed to lend Oldwick Quimby's warthog.

When the fire engine clanged back to the pier, Allegra was still in her place blocking the gangplank. Even before the engine stopped, Wallace Warthog, the pride of Quimby, had spotted Allegra with all her beautiful whiskers and warts. With a joyous grunt he leaped form his perch behind the hoses and scampered up the gangplank.

For Wallace it was love at first sight. Never had
Wallace seen such lovely whiskers and warts.

No one ever forgot that kiss.
"Beautiful," said some.
"A true welcome," said others.
"A kiss for a warthog!" everyone said.

Long after the passengers had left the ship, Allegra and Wallace stood gazing into each other's eyes. It was obvious to the officials of Oldwick and Quimby that Wallace and Allegra must never be parted. Oldwick and Quimby must share these noble creatures.

33

And so the good people of Oldwick and Quimby began
to build a fine new zoo between the towns.

The spirit of goodwill caught on. The housewives of
Oldwick and Quimby baked cakes for the sake of baking
cakes and often exchanged recipes.

Baseball games were famous for good sportsmanship and courtesy.

And it was a very good thing that they had decided to share the warthog couple. Spring came and a beautiful warthog baby arrived.

And no one–not even the mayors–could have figured
how to divide three evenly.